WHERE'S THAT BONE?

by Lucille Recht Penner
Illustrated by Lynn Adams

The Kane Press
New York

Book Design/Art Direction: Roberta Pressel

Library of Congress Cataloging-in-Publication Data

Penner, Lucille Recht.
    Where's that bone?/Lucille Recht Penner; illustrated by Lynn Adams.
      p. cm. — (Math matters.)
    Summary: Jill uses a map to keep track of the places where her dog Bingo has been burying his bones to save them from being taken by Hulk the cat.
      ISBN: 978-1-57565-097-5 (pbk. : alk. paper)
      [1. Maps—Fiction. 2. Dogs—Fiction. 3. Bones—Fiction. 4. Cats—Fiction.]
      I. Adams, Lynn (Lynn Joan), ill. II. Title. III. Series.
PZ7.P38465 Wh 2000
[E]—dc21   99-088840
                                                                                        CIP
                                                                                         AC

ISBN 978-1-57565-591-8 (e-book)

10

First published in the United States of America in 2000 by Kane Press, Inc.
Printed at Worzalla Publishing, Stevens Point, WI, U.S.A., February 2013.

MATH MATTERS is a registered trademark of Kane Press, Inc.

Visit us online at **www.kanepress.com**

 Like us on Facebook
facebook.com/kanepress

 Follow us on Twitter
@kanepress

"Let's go, Bingo!" Jill shouted every morning. Then she and her dog, Bingo, would go for a walk around the block. When they got home, Jill always gave Bingo a bone. Bingo loved bones.

One day Jill's Aunt Sally came to stay
for a while. She brought her cat, Hulk.
Bingo was scared of Hulk.

Hulk jumped on Bingo.

He ate his food.

He even grabbed Bingo's toys.

The only good thing about Hulk was
that he slept a lot. He took a very long
nap every afternoon.

The day after Hulk came, Bingo didn't eat his bone. Instead, he buried it outside in the yard. Jill saw him through the window.

"Why is he doing that?" Jill asked
her mother.
"I think he's hiding it from Hulk,"
she said.

"Don't worry," Jill told Bingo. "Cats don't eat bones." Bingo just sighed and put his head on his paws.

Later that day Hulk took his afternoon nap. "Dig up your bone now," Jill said. "You can eat it while Hulk is inside sleeping."

Bingo dug here and there. But he couldn't remember where he had buried his bone.

The same thing happened the next day. And the day after that. Bingo buried his bones. Then he couldn't find them.

Bingo kept losing all his bones. How could Jill help him?

She thought and thought. At last she had it. She made a big map of her backyard.

The next time Jill and Bingo came
back from a walk, Jill climbed up into
her treehouse.

"Mom!" she called. "Will you give
Bingo a bone?"

"Sure," her mother called back.

Jill watched Bingo. He carried his bone
behind the bird feeder and looked around.

Finally Bingo buried it in front of the
bush with the pink flowers.
Jill marked the place on her map.

The next day, Bingo got another bone. He went around and around the turtle pond. He sniffed the air. Then he circled the apple tree. Bingo buried the bone between the tree and a rock.

Jill made an X on her map to the right of the apple tree.

All at once Jill jumped. Hulk had
leaped into the treehouse. Jill knew cats
can't read maps, but she covered it up
anyway, just in case.

Luckily, at that moment Aunt Sally called, "Hulkie! Time for a treat!"

"Thank goodness," Jill said, as Hulk ran back down the tree.

The next day Bingo dug a hole in front
of the porch. He put in his new bone. But
when he saw Hulk, he took it out again.

Bingo ran over the bridge to the
flower garden. Uh-oh. But it was okay.
Only one flower got bent when he
buried the bone again.

Bingo carried the next bone all over the yard. Suddenly, he dashed behind the swing. He made a left turn and buried the bone under the tree where Jill was sitting.

Jill showed Bingo her map. She had
marked an X for every bone. It would be
easy to find them after Hulk and Aunt
Sally left. If they *ever* left.

At last Aunt Sally was ready to go home. "Goodbye," Jill called. Bingo wagged his tail hard.

"Bye," said Aunt Sally.

"Meow," said Hulk.

I ♥ CATS

The next day Jill and Bingo took a nice
long walk. When they got home, Bingo
wanted a bone. Jill could tell. She took out
her map. "Let's go find one," she said.

Yay! Hurray! The bone was right where
Jill had put the mark on her map. Right
under the tree.

The map worked! Every day they dug
up another bone. But the last bone was
missing. All they found was an empty hole.

Bingo looked around. Jill knew he
thought Hulk had taken it. But she was
sure cats didn't eat bones. Or did they?

A week later, Jill got a letter from Aunt Sally. There was a picture of Hulk in it. And guess what he was holding?

Bingo's bone!

"You were right, Bingo," Jill said. "I guess cats *do* like bones. Do you think they read maps, too?"

POSITION CHART

In each picture, Bingo is hiding from Hulk.
Where is Bingo?

left of the tree

right of the bucket

under the blanket

on the swing

inside the house

outside the garage

behind the fence

between the bushes